THE BULLY BROTHERS

TRICK THE TOOTH FAIRY

LIBRARY
Concrete Elementary School
Concrete, WA

A Grosset & Dunlap **ALL ABOARD BOOK**™

For bullies everywhere—to meet the world with love —M.T.

For P.J.—because you let me bully my way into your heart—J.L.

Text copyright © 1993 by Mike Thaler. Illustrations copyright © 1993 by Jared Lee. All rights reserved. Published by Grosset & Dunlap, Inc., which is a member of The Putnam & Grosset Group, New York. ALL ABOARD BOOKS is a trademark of The Putnam & Grosset Group. THE LITTLE ENGINE THAT COULD and engine design are trademarks of Platt & Munk, Publishers, a division of Grosset & Dunlap, Inc. Published simultaneously in Canada. Printed in the U.S.A.

Library of Congress Cataloging-in-Publication Data
Thaler, Mike, 1936-   The Bully Brothers trick the Tooth Fairy / by Mike Thaler ; illustrated by Jared Lee.   p.   cm. — (All aboard books)   Summary: When Bubba and Bumpo find out that they can get money from the Tooth Fairy for any teeth they put under their pillows, they hatch a scheme to make themselves rich. [1. Tooth Fairy—Fiction. 2. Teeth—Fiction. 3. Moneymaking projects—Fiction.]   I. Lee, Jared., ill.   II. Title.   III. Series.   PZ7.T3Bv 1993
[E]—dc20 92-72834 CIP AC ISBN 0-448-40519-9
      C D E F G H I J

THE BULLY BROTHERS

TRICK THE TOOTH FAIRY

by MIKE THALER
illustrated by JARED LEE

Grosset & Dunlap, Publishers

Bubba and Bumpo were always on the lookout for an easy way to make some money.

But when they both lost a tooth, and their mother told them to put the teeth under their pillows for the Tooth Fairy, they had no idea what would happen.

"Thithy thuff," said Bubba.

"Baby thuff," said Bumpo.

Much to their surprise, when they awoke, the teeth were gone. And there were silver dollars in their place!

Bubba looked at Bumpo. Bumpo looked at Bubba. They both ran to the mirror and counted their teeth.

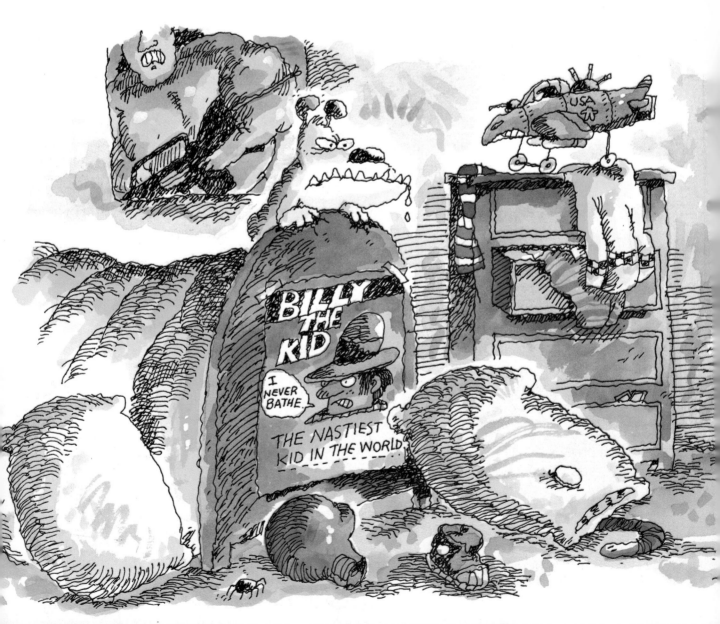

"I have twenty-three," said Bubba.
"I have twenty-three, too," said Bumpo.
"That's *FORTY-SIX DOLLARS!*" said Bubba.
"Get the hammer," said Bumpo.

"Wait," said Bubba, scratching his crew cut.
"Wait?" said Bumpo, scratching his.
"How many friends do we have?"
"None," said Bumpo.

"Okay, how many kids do we know?"
"Lots," said Bumpo, beginning to see the light.
"They all have *teeth*!" said Bubba.
The Bully Brothers gave each other a high five.

LIBRARY
Concrete Elementary School
Concrete, WA

Then they put on their purple leather jackets with the ten-inch fringe, got on their "Li'l Hawg" bikes, and cruised the neighborhood.

They looked into the mouth of every kid they met.

They listened.
They watched.

Then they pounced.

"What's the matter?" they asked Rodney Fish.
"My tooth is looth," said Rodney.
"Oh my," said Bubba.
"Oh my," said Bumpo.
"Have some taffy," said Bubba.
"Gee, thankth," said Rodney.
Rodney bit down.

Bubba and Bumpo yanked the taffy. Out popped Rodney's tooth.

"Give me my tooth!" cried Rodney.

"It's in *our* taffy," said Bubba as they pedaled away. That night they put Rodney's tooth under the pillow. And the next morning they found another silver dollar.

At school they circled the cafeteria on tooth patrol. They found Cynthia Melnick eating applesauce.

"Loose tooth?" said Bubba.

"Yeth," said Cynthia.

"Too bad you can't eat," said Bumpo.

"Here, have some bubble gum," said Bubba. They each gave Cynthia five pieces. She put them all in her mouth and chewed.

"Let's see you blow a bubble," said Bubba.
Cynthia blew hard, and in the big bubble was her tooth.

Bumpo popped the bubble, and Bubba caught the tooth.
That night it went under the pillow.

"The Tooth Fairy's going to get suspicious," said Bumpo.

Bubba went to his treasure chest and came back with some black wax.

"Put this over your teeth," he said. "Then it'll look like you've lost more."

As business improved, the row of black wax spread across Bumpo's mouth.

"It looks like a black hole in space," said Bubba.
Soon Bubba had a black hole, too. Business was great.
But then they got greedy.

"Where do people with loose teeth go?" asked Bubba.
"To the dentist!" said Bumpo.
So the Bully Brothers put on white coats, grabbed a bag of disguise stuff, and pedaled over to Doctor Molar's office.

They found an empty room. Bumpo lost the toss, so he had to be the nurse.

He put on a red wig and went into the waiting room.

"The dentist will see you now," he said to the old lady who was sitting there.

Mrs. Applegate followed him. She sat down in the chair and took out her false teeth.

"Bingo!" shouted Bubba.

"Bingo!" shouted Bumpo as he grabbed the teeth and ran for the door.

Mrs. Applegate screamed as best she could.

In ran Doctor Molar.

Out the door shot Bubba and Bumpo in their long white coats. Doctor Molar ran after them. Mrs. Applegate ran after Doctor Molar.

They nearly got away, but at the top of the stairs, Bubba tripped over his white coat, Bumpo tripped over Bubba, Mrs. Applegate's teeth went flying, and the Bully Brothers rolled over and over, hitting their teeth on every step all the way downstairs.

Soon Doctor Molar stood over them. "Alright, boys, hand over the teeth!"

Bubba spit out some teeth in his hand. So did Bumpo.

"Not those teeth," said Doctor Molar.

"Theeth teeth!" shouted Mrs. Applegate. They were in the potted palm.

As it all turned out, Bubba lost three teeth, Bumpo lost four, and Mrs. Applegate lost five—which had to be replaced.

The bill came to exactly forty-six dollars. So from then on instead of putting silver dollars under their pillows, the Tooth Fairy sent a check to Doctor Molar.

"Thith ith not the American way," said Bubba sadly, lifting up his pillow.

"No," said Bumpo, hitting Bubba with his.